SUMMER OLYMPICS

By Mark Littleton

ZondervanPublishingHouse
Grand Rapids, Michigan

A Division of HarperCollins*Publishers*

Summer Olympics
Copyright © 1996 by Mark Littleton

Requests for information should be addressed to:

⛪ ZondervanPublishingHouse
Grand Rapids, Michigan 49530

Library of Congress Cataloging-in-Publication Data

Littleton, Mark R.
    Summer Olympics: Mark Littleton.
        p. cm. — (Sports heroes)
    Summary: Athletes who have competed in different summer Olympics
give their testimony to the power of faith in their lives.
    ISBN: 0-310-20266-3 (softcover)
    1. Athletes—United States—Biography—Juvenile literature.   2.
Athletes—Religious life—United States—Juvenile literature.   3.
Olympics—Juvenile literature. [1. Athletes.   2. Christian life.   3.
Olympics.] I. Title. II. Series: Littleton, Mark R., 1950–   Sports heroes.
GV697.A1L585   1996
796.'092'2—dc20   96-2351
                                            CIP
                                            AC

Edited by Tom Raabe
Interior design by Joe Vriend

Printed in the United States of America

96 97 98 99 00 01 02 /❖ DH/ 10 9 8 7 6 5 4 3 2

For Mom, who still cheers to the TV screen when the summer Olympics are rolling.

Thanks to Sam Mings of Lay Witnesses for Christ for helping me connect with Joe DeLoach and Carl Lewis.

Also, thanks to Dave Branon of Sports Spectrum Magazine for his leads on Brian Diemer, Madeline Mims, and Josh Davis.

Contents

Meet Summer's Olympic Heroes

For any world-class athlete, the Olympics are the ultimate.

The ultimate arena in which to perform. The ultimate joy in life. The ultimate high on the field of trial.

For the Christian athlete, they're also an ultimate gift from God.

Few athletes make it as far as the Olympics. Each country in the world is allowed to send only its top three athletes for each event. That means, of the thousands of athletes in the United States, only *three* per event will make it to the Olympics.

And even fewer win medals in the Olympics. The three Americans who qualify in each event will compete with a hundred athletes for three medals in that event. And those hundred are the best athletes the world has to offer.

The United States always sends a full roster to the Olympics, and 1996 will be no different. Several of the athletes you'll read about in these pages might be there: Jackie Joyner-Kersee, Joe DeLoach, Carl Lewis, Josh Davis, and Brian Diemer. Madeline Manning Mims will probably be there as an encourager, chaplain, and spectator who has already made her mark.

Above all, every one of these athletes will go as Christ's special messenger. Perhaps they will gain opportunities that only world-class athletes can hope for.

Think about it: The Olympics are not only a great athletic and media event, but they're a prime opportunity for God to work and raise up new missionaries for His work in countries all over the world.

As you read these pages, don't just marvel, don't just wish. Do something else as well: pray. God will work through your prayers, and you'll be there, too.

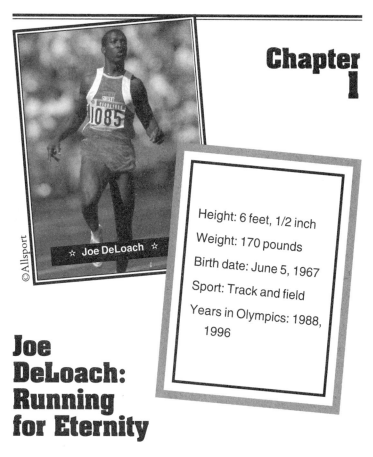

©Allsport

☆ Joe DeLoach ☆

Height: 6 feet, 1/2 inch

Weight: 170 pounds

Birth date: June 5, 1967

Sport: Track and field

Years in Olympics: 1988, 1996

Joe DeLoach: Running for Eternity

Joe DeLoach says he was the "caboose" of his very big family. How big a family? Eleven sisters and one brother. All older.

"So," he says, "when I was young, I ran. I always had someone after me, a brother, a sister. So I learned to run early. And I was good at it."

Joe played baseball and football in school, and also ran track. He usually won the footraces. "When we had field days in elementary school, I always won the short events. I was always the fastest kid on the block, fastest kid in school."

He excelled in summer track programs, too. But running wasn't always his chief interest.

"Running took me by surprise. My goal was to be a pro football player. I was a wide receiver. I didn't have the greatest hands, but I could beat the opponents. However, I had a coach in high school, also a Christian. His name was Marshall Brown. He was the football coach as well. About that time, the 1984 Olympics at Los Angeles were coming. I was a junior in high school and was on the football team. Coach Brown said to me, 'Joe, pay attention to a guy out of the University of Houston. His name is Carl Lewis. He is going for four gold medals.'"

That's exactly what Carl Lewis did. And Joe had something to shoot for.

Coach Brown had gotten Joe's attention. He told Joe he could make a career out of running. After watching the 1984 Olympics, Joe went to the Bahamas to participate in the Junior Olympics and came home with three gold medals: 100 meters, 200 meters, and the 4 X 100 relay. People began comparing him to Carl Lewis, saying he would be the next one to beat that great track star. Joe wasn't sure he believed it, but the idea fermented in his mind.

Joe had made the varsity track team at Bay City (Texas) High School already in ninth grade. He decided to try out for the relay team because everyone said he could make it. Joe tried out for first leg, the second most important position on a relay team. Bay City's team ran a senior who played defensive end for the football team. A big bruiser of a fellow who towered over little Joe.

"We ran in the tryouts and I beat him. Bad. I was terrified. I thought the guy would come along and beat the tar out of me. But he didn't. In fact, he seemed kind of amazed. I made first leg of the team and ran varsity the whole year."

He broke plenty of freshman records in the sprints. The record he set in the fifteen-year-old nationals still stands today: 10.0 in the 100 meters. He also set a record of 20.4 in the 200 meters, but it only stood for one day.

"I don't know how good the times are," he says. "I mean, I never put much stock in the numbers. I have never run that fast again in those races, and it's possible the times weren't as exact as later times when I ran in the Olympics and other places.

Joe took away all the honors in his district and posted many meet records. He was named all-American both his junior and senior years.

After high school, though, he ran into some serious problems with college recruiting. He wanted to attend the University of Houston where Carl Lewis and Kirke Baptiste, another sprinter on the 1984 gold-medal relay team, had run.

Houston coach Tom Tellez came down to Bay City to recruit Joe for track and field. At the time, Joe was thinking more about football. So Coach Tellez said he'd wait for Joe to decide. Joe was something of a celebrity in his hometown, and everyone wanted to know whether he'd be the man to defeat Carl Lewis in the 100. Many people were following the story.

Finally, Joe made an announcement in the newspaper that he wasn't going to play football. He wanted to make his mark in track.

Coach Tellez learned about the decision and came to visit Joe and his family, bringing Carl Lewis and Kirke Baptiste with him.

"Everyone in my family showed up—cousins, aunts, uncles—to meet the famed duo of Lewis and Baptiste. I was amazed myself. They talked to me about the program. We were all crammed into our home and everyone met Carl. The thing that struck me about Carl was that he was so down-to-earth. He acted like he'd known my family all his life. I started asking him questions about running fast. He told me I had the talent, and if I worked hard I could accomplish the same things he'd accomplished. How often do you get to train beside the greatest athlete in track and field history? I decided I wanted to come down to Houston to see the facility and everything."

That's precisely what Joe did. But suddenly he found himself embroiled in a huge controversy. The NCAA (National Collegiate Athletic Association) rules said that using Carl and Kirke to recruit Joe was a violation. In the end, the NCAA declared that Joe couldn't receive a scholarship from Houston because of the violation.

Joe was devastated. His family could not afford to send him to college without a scholarship.

The strange thing was, he could have taken a scholarship to any other school in the United States—and plenty offered him one. But no other school had Coach Tellez, who had coached several Olympians, as well as Carl Lewis, the four-time gold-medal winner. Joe longed to go to Houston. So he decided to go anyway—on faith and on the conviction that God wanted him there.

He was allowed to train at the track, but not with the team. However, Joe and his family pleaded their case in court and won. So, although he had to sit out his first year, he was eligible the next year, received a scholarship, and ran for the University of Houston.

Joe only ran two years for Houston, starting in 1986. He had to sit out his sophomore year because of hamstring trouble. But his junior year, he won the conference championship and placed fourth in the nationals in the 200 meters. He ran the fastest time he'd ever run in the 100 after high school, 10.01 seconds, which placed him number one in the world at the time, for that year. He wasn't ranked in the 200 meters that year, even though he had once run 19.9.

Next on the agenda for Joe was the Olympic Trials. He went into them with the two fastest times in the world in the 100 and 200.

"I finished in fifth place in the 100. I was disappointed, but I ended up as an alternate, and had a shot to make the relay." He did make the cut for the 200, though, and in the Olympics, would have a chance to run against his hero, Carl Lewis.

Joe hustled into the 1988 Olympics in really high spirits. Carl Lewis suggested to him that they get their own place instead of living at the Olympic Village. Carl felt they'd have more privacy and also have the time to train the way they wanted. Carl had been under a lot of pressure in 1984. The constant stress of facing the press, answering questions, and dealing with the many ups and downs of the Olympics wore on a quiet person like Carl. So Carl made private arrangements.

"We stayed in a private home," Joe says. "I could ask Carl a lot of questions. It gave me an unprecedented amount of focus. We worked out. We did some things with Lay Witnesses for Christ, sharing our testimony and preaching and so on. One night we did something they called 'An Evening with the Stars.' We gathered a lot of the top athletes at the Olympics who were Christians and gave our testimonies in church. A lot of people ended up getting saved."

Joe's pastor, Dr. Michael P. Williams, often told him, "God gives us celebrity to win people to the kingdom." So Joe's group of Christian Olympians went to the largest church in Seoul, Korea, Dr. Cho's church.

"These people were drawn to our celebrity," says Joe. "Many of those people probably wanted to be like us. So we told our stories. We told them how Jesus changed our lives and made the difference. It was beautiful."

Joe had learned about Jesus and salvation from his earliest years and became a Christian when he was eight or nine years old. The family attended a church called Bible Days Revival that was within walking distance of the house. His parents were saved first, then they introduced all the children to the gospel.

After one of Joe's eleven sisters, Honey, went down and turned her life over to Christ, Joe says, "She came home all excited. She was a different person. Someone had lit a torch under her. I wasn't really that excited about it at that point. It was the kind of church with a lot of shouting and people in a frenzy. I wasn't used to that. I thought the people were crazy. So I didn't want anything to do with it. I was a little embarrassed.

"One night the speaker started to prophesy—actually tell things about a person that no one knew. He called my mother forward. Then he told her to stay in that spot where she stood. I was sitting in the balcony watching. This speaker hurried up into the balcony and dropped a handkerchief down from where he stood. It hit my mom's head. The moment it hit, she fell down like she was dead. I was terrified. I started screaming in the balcony that they'd killed my mother. It was a real scene. Finally, someone explained what had happened to my mom, and that was when I believed."

However, Joe wasn't very committed. He heard the Word of God and went to church, but it wasn't until he was twelve that he became sold on the idea.

"I liked playing the drums. I played on pots and pans. Just pounding away. My parents told me they'd get me a set of drums if I played them in the church. That excited me. So they bought me the drums and I started playing in church all the time. I got to the point where I couldn't wait for church to open. I got saturated with the Word. And I heard the story. Gradually, it all soaked in. I learned to live by faith."

By the time the 1988 Olympics came around, Joe had learned a lot about living for the Lord. He frequently spoke at sports events organized by Sam Mings and Lay Witnesses for Christ. Carl Lewis also spoke at such events, and Joe and Carl became close. But that didn't change the fact that the two friends were also competitors. Joe ran the same events as Carl and would compete against him in the 200 meters in Seoul. Joe thought a lot about that

18

event. This was the greatest chance and match of his life. Could he beat Carl Lewis, the favorite?

As Joe faced that question, he thought about something that had happened years before, a prayer he'd prayed while he was in high school.

"The church I grew up in had taught me many things about Christ. I really believed if we asked God for something, He would do it. So I asked God to use my talents in track and field. There were three things I wanted: a college education, to see the world, and to win an Olympic gold medal. So I began praying for those three things in high school.

"My junior year, after I had seen Carl Lewis win four gold medals in 1984 and then when I also won three golds in the Junior Olympics, I came back from the Bahamas full of faith. I told my friends on the track team, 'I'll be the next guy to beat Carl Lewis.' What a big mistake! Some of these guys thought I was crazy already for the church I went to.

"During my senior year, I had an amazing streak of answered prayers. I broke so many records at meets it was amazing. In the 4 X 100 relay, we'd be fifteen meters behind. I was the anchor of the relay, and the third guy, when he handed off the baton, would say, 'Go get 'em, Joe.' I'd spring out and catch up. I got to be a celebrity in town. Kids

19

would ask me for my autograph. It was at that time that I did something I would later forget. I had this dream of winning the gold medal. So I would write on those autographs 'Joe DeLoach, Seoul, '88.' People would ask me what this meant. I told them it meant I'd be in the Olympics and I'd win the gold. I guess I was really putting my neck out, but a lot of those people remembered."

So, could he beat Carl Lewis in the 200 meters?

"As I prayed about the race and read the Scriptures, I began to get a picture of what was going to happen. I saw the finish line and me crossing it. I wanted to run 19.6.

"Then the race came. Carl was in lane three or so. I got a great start out of the blocks. I was in lane six. Carl went past me in the turn. Everyone else was watching Carl and me. I remember when he passed me—normally I would get a little worried about that. He was about ten meters ahead of me. But I had this peace in my heart. I knew it would be all right. I'd catch him. It was like I was just floating. I caught him about halfway through the race. He looked over at me. I knew I would beat him then. I ran 19.75, an American and an Olympic record, tying Carl's own record. Carl got the silver. I won the gold. He would have a flawless Olympic career except for that silver."

That brings us back to that autograph Joe used to give—"Joe DeLoach, Seoul, '88."

Bay City arranged for a big homecoming for Joe after the Olympics. They called it "Joe DeLoach Day." Joe says, "People lined up for autographs. The line went right out of the stadium. Back at the end of the line were three or four young people who came up to me all happy and excited. They had tears in their eyes. They were just waiting to get to me. I was about to sign for them when they said, 'We already got your autograph. We got it in 1985 when you were a senior in high school and you wrote, "Joe DeLoach, Seoul, '88." And now you've done it.'"

That really hit him! He had forgotten about signing autographs that way. And suddenly he realized that God had answered all three of the prayers he had prayed way back in high school. He had asked that God get him to college, permit him to see the world, and allow him to win a gold medal in the Olympics.

Today, he has a college degree, he's been to over twenty countries, and an Olympic gold medal is draped around his neck, with a record to boot.

How does the Olympics affect a person's life? "It gives you the feeling that you're special. People recognize the level of commitment it takes to win a gold medal. Since winning the gold medal, I've been speaking at companies and schools that I'd never have had a chance to speak to. I'm not known like Carl is. But it's still become a powerful witnessing tool. I'm using that celebrity status to change the lives of other people."

Joe has had recurring health problems, which kept him from competing in the 1992 Barcelona Olympics and have prohibited him from running regularly. But he has a great peace about what he's accomplished. He hopes to make it to the 1996 Olympics despite the problems. So maybe God will give him another opportunity.

But even if He doesn't, Joe knows God is with him in what he's doing. Because he's running for eternity and for God's kingdom, not just for himself.

Chapter 2

★ Carl Lewis ★

©Allsport

Height: 6 feet, 2 inches

Weight: 175 pounds

Birth date: July 1, 1961

Sport: Track and field

Years in Olympics: 1984, 1988, 1992, 1996

Carl Lewis: Legend-Maker and Legend-Breaker

They come along about once a century.

Or at the very most, once a decade.

Athletes like Jim Thorpe, Eric Liddell, Jesse Owens, who accomplish feats the world has never seen before.

Every now and then someone turns the track world upside down.

23

One such athlete is Carl Lewis. He stands alone among track and field and Olympic competitors. Today, he is poised to compete in his fourth Olympics. It would be his fifth, but the United States boycotted the 1980 Olympics. (The Soviet Union had recently invaded Afghanistan, and President Carter wanted to send a message that the United States would not stand by and do nothing.)

What is more, this man is a committed Christian. He speaks frequently for Lay Witnesses for Christ, an evangelistic organization that uses top athletes to spread the good news of Christ. In 1981, he heard a man named Sam Mings preach the gospel at a chapel during an NCAA championships meet, and he accepted Jesus on the spot. He knew he needed the Lord. And Jesus has guided him ever since.

How did this incredible young man get his start?

Two years after his birth in Birmingham, Alabama, his parents moved to Willingboro, New Jersey, where they took over the coaching positions of the boys' and girls' track teams at the high school there. Carl's two older brothers excelled in athletics, but Carl himself was small and skinny. Everyone in the Lewis family considered him the runt.

That didn't deter Carl from playing baseball or leaping off the porch to practice his long jump. In fact, he first began long jumping at age nine while his father was building a patio. The sand he poured as a foundation became the "pit," and Carl long-jumped to his heart's content. Everyone joked about it, but Carl took it seriously and worked hard. Over the years, Carl accumulated a vast internal library of knowledge about technique. Many long jumpers start late in their teens, after devoting most of their training to short-distance running, but Carl learned long jumping technique early and later developed his own variation called the "double-hitch kick." We'll look at that in a moment.

By the time Carl reached high school, he had filled out some, grown several inches, and become an able competitor. In tenth grade, he regularly jumped over 22 feet and ran the 100-yard dash in less than ten seconds. After high school, in the 1979 Pan American Games, he won a bronze medal in the long jump with a leap of 26 feet, 8 1/4 inches. He and his sister, Carol, who also excelled in the long jump, both made the 1980 Olympic team but weren't able to compete because the United States boycotted the Olympics that year.

When it came time for college, there was only one place Carl wanted to go: the University of Houston. That was largely because of the university's track coach, Tom Tellez, already known as a nurturer of great athletes. In Carl's freshman year he won the long jump in the NCAA Outdoor Track and Field Championships. People were taking notice of this new star, and many saw him as a true contender.

Carl's coach helped him zero in on a problem that had dogged Carl since his early teens. He had been jumping on a bad right knee for years. Frequently after a competition, he found himself laid up, nursing a swollen knee and fighting the pain. After various tests and examinations, the doctors found that Carl suffered from "jumpers knee," a condition common in jumpers and known in medical terms as patella tendonitis. Scar tissue from a fall Carl took at age eleven was rubbing against the tendons in his knee.

The doctors ordered therapy and exercise, and told Carl to learn a new jumping technique that put less strain on the knee. That technique, which became known as the double-hitch kick, involves a longer than normal approach to the takeoff board. For Carl it was 171 feet, or 23 strides. When he hit the board, he was sprinting at 27 miles an hour. While in the air, he pumped his legs two and a half more times as if he were still running, and windmilled his arms backward. All this motion kept him from falling over backward! It took pressure off his knee, too, because he didn't jump as high.

Just as his jumping style astonished observers, so it established him as the premiere long jumper of his time. In 1982, he was ranked number one in the long jump and the 100-meter dash. By late 1983, he had long-jumped over 28 feet fourteen times. And his longest jump—28 feet, 10 1/2 inches—was only

4 inches shy of Bob Beamon's super leap of 29 feet, 2 1/2 inches in Mexico City in 1968.

Carl won the 1981 Sullivan Award as the United States's greatest amateur athlete and, in 1982, received the Jesse Owens Award for the outstanding track and field athlete. When anyone thought of writing about sprinting or long jumping, Carl's name was the first to spring to mind. He seemed unbeatable.

In 1983, he ran the 100 meters in less than ten seconds (9.97), and the 200 in a U.S. record of 19.75. Then in the U.S. National Championships, he won all three events he competed in—the 100, the 200, and the long jump. No one had done a "triple" like that since the 1880s.

As Carl Lewis's star rose, the media scrutinized him intensely. What they found was—they thought—an arrogant grandstander who liked to hotdog after a big victory. But inside, Carl was a quiet, composed thinker, always analyzing, always trying to improve. He did not give interviews like other athletes, and some called him aloof. Those who knew Carl well, though, understood him as an intensely religious man, committed to his sports, his family, and his Lord. For him competition was the main thing, not media attention. "Competition is the foremost thing to me, competition and the fun of it. Everything else comes after."

That competitive edge put Carl in a spotlight brighter than he'd ever been in before. The 1984

Olympics were coming, and Carl had qualified for four events—the 100, 200, 4 X 100 relay, and long jump. To win all four was called an impossible feat. Only one man in history had done it: Jesse Owens, in the 1936 Olympics. Carl Lewis was shooting for it, though, and all the world watched.

Carl runs the 100 meters unlike most champions. Most runners look for a great start, then gather speed for the first forty meters. From that point on, when they've reached maximum stride, speed, and effort, it's all out. In other words, most sprinters strive to get ahead and then stay ahead.

With Carl, though, the first fifty meters are almost a write-off. He doesn't try to get ahead. In fact, he lays back. But at fifty meters, Carl explodes, catches the field, and then speeds past them like a magnum bullet.

That's precisely what he did in the 1984 Olympics. Laying back, as if taunting the other runners, Carl detonated at fifty meters and blew away the field with a 9.99 showing.

Two days later, Carl took the gold in the long jump with a leap of 28 feet, 1/4 inch. He achieved that on his first try. To avoid injury in the chilly weather of Los Angeles, he didn't even take his next four jumps. He felt confident that first jump would bowl over the rest of the contenders. And it did.

Next on the Lewis agenda was the 200 meters. Once again, he showed the field what he was made of and took it all in a time of 19.80 seconds, an Olympic record.

Finally, there was the 4 X 100-meter relay. As the fastest man alive, Carl naturally ran the anchor leg. The team took the gold with an Olympic- and world-record time of 37.83 seconds.

Carl had accomplished the unthinkable. Four golds in the same Olympics. Same as Jesse Owens in 1936.

Some might be tempted to think that Carl Lewis is little more than a machine cranking out record times and distances. But Carl has numerous interests apart from athletics, one of which is music. In fact, he cut a record before the Olympics, called "Going for the Gold," that was something of a hit in Europe. He also took acting lessons in New York, thinking that one day he might divide his attention between sports and Hollywood.

Sports, however, was Carl's focus in 1985. That year he followed up his stellar Olympic showing with more of the same, capturing his forty-second consecutive long jump competition. He remained the man to beat in both the sprints and the long jump.

Then in 1988, another turn came at the Olympics, this one in Seoul, South Korea. Would Carl win four more golds?

It didn't look that way at first. In the 100 meters, Carl was bested by Ben Johnson of Canada. Carl ran a new American record of 9.92.

But then a strange twist of fate occurred. Johnson's tests for drugs came in, and the authorities discovered he'd been using illegal steroids. He was disqualified, the gold went to Carl, and his 9.92 seconds became the time to beat. Now, not only was it an American record, it became the new Olympic record.

Carl next won the long jump with a leap of 28 feet, 7 1/2 inches. It was Carl's fifty-sixth straight victory in the long jump, a consecutive win streak that no one has bettered before or since.

Next up was the 200 meters, and Carl had a fight on his hands. His closest competition was Joe DeLoach, also a Christian (and also in this book). Carl and Joe were friends. They trained together under the same coach at the University of Houston (Tom Tellez), and they had won many honors together. Both wanted to run well, both wanted to set records, and both wanted to win. Carl had an Olympic record and a chance to repeat in the 200. But Joe had something more, perhaps something greater: this might be his only Olympic showing in his whole life.

The 200 meters presents a special challenge. The runners go around one bend in the track. In a full sprint, that's difficult and takes tremendous training to perfect. In such a race and with two such athletes, anything could happen. What did happen was little short of amazing.

Going into the bend, Joe was a little behind Carl. But as they came around the turn, Joe caught up. Carl shot Joe a look, then poured it on. But Joe poured it on just a little more. At the end, Joe won, tying Carl's American 200-meter record of 19.75 and setting a new Olympic record, too.

So it turned out to be a great day for Christians, any way you cut it.

The fourth event, the 4 X 100-meter relay, should have been a cakewalk. However, Carl's team was disqualified for an illegal pass of the baton. No gold for any American in that event.

All told, Carl took home two golds and a silver from the 1988 Olympics. He now had six gold medals and a silver during his Olympic competitions, and ranked up there with Jim Thorpe and Jesse Owens as an Olympic legend. In fact, he was in a class all his own.

And still, Carl wasn't done. In 1991, Carl jumped 29 feet, his best long jump ever, and he competed in what some have called the greatest 100 meters ever raced.

Let's set the scene. The year was 1991. The event was the World Track and Field Championships in Tokyo, Japan. The setting was a beautiful track, inside a huge stadium that was crammed to capacity.

As the eight men lined up to run the 100 meters, Carl and his closest rival, Leroy Burrell, felt relaxed. Burrell was the favorite. He'd run the two fastest 100s in the last two years and also the most recent 9.90, the world record at the time. Carl was thirty years old. Some thought he had to slow down pretty soon. He was working for a Houston radio station and also plugging his autobiography, and hadn't had much time for training. Some thought he might be out of shape.

These two men were friends. They came out of the same school, had the same coach, and underwent the same training regimen. They now trained at the same club, the Santa Monica Track Club. And their mothers sat together in the stands.

In the quarterfinals, Carl got a bad start but flew by everyone to post a 9.80, the third-fastest time ever recorded. Nonetheless, the wind was up, over the allowable two meters per second, so it was not a world record.

Carl remained hot in the semifinals. With no wind he clocked in at 9.93, only .03 over Burrell's world record of only months before. In real terms, .03 seconds is only the blink of an eye, less than a full step in 100 meters. Everyone knew the world record might be broken.

Leroy Burrell, posting a 9.94 in the semifinals, remained the main contender against Carl. Both athletes were cruising like never before, ready for the greatest race in history.

Then they reached the finals. Burrell took lane three. Linford Christie, the great British runner who had clocked a 9.99 in the semifinals, stood in lane four. Carl had lane five. Next to him in lane six stood Dennis Mitchell, a Santa Monica teammate of Carl and Burrell who also clocked a 9.99 in the semis.

When the gun sounded, Mitchell exploded out of the blocks, getting a better start than anyone. But after a slight lurch, Burrell accelerated. At twenty meters, four runners led: Burrell, Mitchell, Christie, and Ray Stewart of Jamaica. As usual, Carl Lewis ran a little behind them. That was his style, and not something for the crowd to worry about.

At sixty meters, Carl made his move. He always seemed to fire those blaster rockets at that point, and he caught the pack but not Burrell, who still had a clear lead.

At eighty meters, Carl and Leroy had maxed out. Mitchell and Stewart rocketed right behind them, less than a footstep away. The crowd thundered around them. All eight men were sprinting for times never seen before. A new record would probably be set, and it would go to either Carl Lewis or Leroy Burrell.

With ten meters left, Leroy and Carl leaned for the tape. Stride for stride. Neck and neck.

But Carl, at six-two, with those long legs and that magnificent style, had an advantage. He let out his kick and gave it his last bit of energy. Burrell couldn't see him because he was blind in his right eye. He had no idea where Carl was, or how close.

Then suddenly, Leroy realized Carl and he were neck and neck. Both men leaned out.

Ninety-five meters. Five to go. Carl leaned out. Leroy pushed himself. But he was beaten. Carl had won in 9.86 seconds. No wind. It was legal. A new world record.

But that wasn't the only amazing feat that day.

Burrell had run a 9.88, breaking his own world record of 9.90 set two months previously. He said, "My goal was the record. And I got it. Somebody just broke it a little ahead of me. Who better to lose the record to than a friend you know you can race again."[1]

But that was not all. Dennis Mitchell took third with a 9.91. The three teammates from Santa Monica had taken one, two, and three.

Other records fell as well. Christie established a British, European, and Commonwealth record with his fourth-place 9.92. Frank Fredericks of Namibia took fifth with an African record of 9.95. And sixth-place Stewart set a Jamaican record with 9.96.

Six men finished in under 10.0 seconds. Some called it the race of the century. Carl Lewis had run faster than any human being on earth.

It's the stuff of legend. But that's Carl Lewis, legend-maker and legend-breaker.

---

1. Kenny Moore, "The Great Race," *Sports Illustrated*, September 2, 1991, 26.

Chapter 3

©Allsport

☆ Jacqueline Joyner-Kersee ☆

Height: 5 feet, 10 inches

Weight: 155 pounds

Birth date: March 3, 1962

Sport: Track and field

Years in Olympics: 1984, 1988, 1992

Jacqueline Joyner-Kersee: The World's Greatest Athlete

There can only be one at a time.

Usually, it's a man.

But not this time.

What am I talking about? Why, the title "world's greatest athlete."

The 1988 Summer Olympics were coming, and Jackie Joyner-Kersee wanted only two things: a gold medal and a world record. But she would fulfill more than her goals—she would also get that much-sought title.

Jackie performed in two sports: the long jump and the heptathlon.

The long jump is simple enough: after sprinting down a straightaway, the jumper pushes off a little board and leaps high and long. The best female jumpers soar more than 22 feet in this event.

The heptathlon is a little more complicated. It's a multi-event competition similar to the men's decathlon, which is ten events. The women's hep-tathlon (from the Greek word *hepta*) consists of seven events unfolding over two consecutive days. Four events are contested on the first day (100-meter hurdles, high jump, shot put, 200-meter run) and three on the second (long jump, javelin, 800-meter run). It's a grueling schedule. The judges award points for each competitor's performance based on a very specific table. After all seven events are completed, they add up the points and hand out the medals.

Jackie had already shown that she was made of world-record stuff when she won the silver medal in the 1984 Olympics in Los Angeles, finishing five points behind the gold medalist, Glynis Nunn of Australia. If Jackie had finished her 200-meter sprint one-third of a second faster, she would have won! And on April 25, 1986, she nearly broke Jane Frederick's American heptathlon record of 6,803 points. However, because of a broken timer, her point total of 6,910 wasn't considered official. She did break Frederick's record in May 1986 with 6,841 points.

But that's getting ahead of things. First, let's consider where this superlative athlete came from.

Jacqueline Joyner was born on March 3, 1962. Her grandmother took such pride in this new little one that she felt something great was afoot. She named the child after President Kennedy's young wife, Jacqueline Kennedy. Jackie, as she came to be called, was the second of four children.

The Joyners were not a wealthy family. They lived in a little unheated bungalow in East St. Louis, Illinois. Sometimes for dinner they ate only bread with a little dollop of mayonnaise to spread on it.

But they never thought of themselves as poor. Jackie's mother insisted that the kids study hard, work to make good grades, and be polite to everyone.

The local recreation center became the focal point of activity for the Joyner children. There, from the age of nine, Jackie went out for track and field, dance, and cheerleading. She and several other girls put together a little dance group they called the Fabulous Dolls.

Coach Nino Fennoy, himself an athlete, ran a track and field program at the center and it gained the reputation as one of the best in the United States. One of Coach Fennoy's heroes was his coach at Tennessee State University, Ed Temple. Temple had coached Wilma Rudolph, a stellar American athlete who won three gold medals at the 1960 Olympics, in the 100 meters, 200 meters, and 4 X 100-meter relay. Coach Fennoy was looking for his own Wilma Rudolph, and he thought Jackie might be that person. She had commitment, she wanted to excel, and she had plenty of talent. So he nurtured her, along with her older brother, Al.

One time when Al was twelve and Jackie ten, Al said he could beat her in a race without even practicing. Jackie took it seriously and worked out. She wanted to win.

The day of the race came, and kids lined the seventy yards of the street where they were to run. When the starter shouted go, Jackie took off. Seventy yards later, Al was eating her dust. He lost! And she won!

At age twelve, Jackie blossomed. Her long gangly legs got under control and her build began to assume that of an athlete. One day, during a period when Jackie was trying many different events in track and field, a coach was building a pit for the long jump. Jackie walked over to watch, then asked if she could try it. He told her to go ahead. She jumped 16 feet, 9 inches, a distance that any high school senior would feel proud of. But Jackie was only twelve. The coach was so astounded he asked her to do it again.

And she did. That was how she got involved in long jumping. From then on, she practiced long jumping off the porch of her house.

Soon she was participating in so many events that Coach Fennoy suggested she try the pentathlon, a five-event competition that was the forerunner of the heptathlon. She threw the shot, which for her age group weighed six pounds, ran the 80-meter hurdles, and high-jumped. By 1976, when she was fourteen, she won her first national championship in the Junior Olympics.

That same year, Jackie watched the 1976 Olympics in Montreal, where Bruce Jenner won the gold in the decathlon. Jackie was in awe at how the crowd cheered Jenner on and how he was called "the world's greatest athlete." She decided then and there she wanted the same thing.

Jackie went on to Lincoln High School in East St. Louis and worked out under Coach Fennoy's careful eye. She led the basketball team to the state championship and also kept up her track skills. She wanted to win a scholarship and attend college, something neither of her parents had been able to do but had dreamed about for their children. She had been named all-state and all-American in both track and basketball, so her chances were excellent.

Then in 1980, she was deemed too good for the Junior Olympics, and was asked to try out for the real Olympics in the long jump.

At the Olympic Trials, she was able to sail 20 feet, 9 3/4 inches, which was good enough for eighth place, but only the top three were chosen for the Olympics. Unfortunately, 1980 was the year the United States boycotted the Olympics because they were to be held in Moscow.

So Jackie set her sights on 1984, the year she won a silver medal and missed the gold by a third of a second.

Now she wanted to get the gold at the 1988 Olympics and break some records.

She had her first taste of breaking records at the Goetzis International Track Meet in Austria in 1986, where her 6,841 points broke the U.S. heptathlon record set by Jane Frederick (6,803). Now it was time to go after the world mark, 6,946 points, set by Sabine Paetz of East Germany in 1984. The question was: could a woman break the 7000-point ceiling? Some said no one would ever break it. But Jackie wanted to work at breaking that mark and the world record.

Moscow hosted the Goodwill Games in July of that year, and Jackie and her new husband, Bob Kersee, also her coach, traveled to Russia to compete.

On July 7, Jackie burned up the track with personal, American, and world bests all over the place. She ran an American best of 12.85 seconds in the 100-meter hurdles; she high-jumped 6 feet, 2 inches, her personal best; and she sprinted the 200 meters in 23.0 seconds, another personal best. At the end of the day, she was on track for a world record, and possibly the 7000-point barrier.

The next day she posted a 23-foot long jump, a world record, and hurled the javelin 163 feet, 4 inches, a personal best.

One more event to go, the 800 meters, perhaps Jackie's most difficult challenge. She needed a time of 2:24.64 to break 7000 points. She took off like a shell from a cannon. When it was over, Jackie shattered that time by more than fourteen seconds: 2:10.02. With that, she established a new world record of 7,148 points for the heptathlon. The announcer, speaking Russian first and then English, said, "It's marvelous. It's magnificent."

Jackie had shattered the 7000-point barrier and set a world record. But she was still hungry; she was gunning for more. Furthermore, some sports commentators said it was a fluke. One said, "No way you're ever doing that again!"

They didn't know Jackie Joyner-Kersee very well. As a Christian, she believed God had a special task for her in the world. She knew God had made her for this time. And she was going to go for it all—for His glory and the glory of America.

In August of that year, 1986, she and her coach-husband set their sights on Houston and the U.S. Olympic Sports Festival. This event is held each year that the Olympics aren't and is designed to give athletes another national competition during off-Olympics years. The temperatures in Houston soared that month to 102 degrees. It was 126 degrees inside the stadium! As Jackie gave news conferences, she sat on two bags of ice!

The heat didn't daunt her spirit, though. She went in, established more records and world bests, and also broke her own world record with 7,158 points. The previous month's victory was no fluke. She had proved it!

At the end of the year, for all these stunning performances, Jackie received the Jesse Owens Memorial Award for outstanding track and field athlete. *Track and Field News* named her Women's Athlete of the Year. And she also beat out David Robinson, basketball hero at the Naval Academy, and Vinnie Testaverde, Heisman Trophy winner, for the prestigious Sullivan Award, given to the most outstanding amateur athlete in the United States. It was only the eighth time in sixty-seven years that the award went to a woman, so it was a double-barreled victory. Not only was Jackie the best woman athlete in the country, but the best athlete of all, both men and women.

That's quite an honor.

In 1987 Jackie continued performing incredibly well as one of the world's greatest athletes.

In the heptathlon, Jackie's strengths were the high jump, 100-meter hurdles, long jump, and 200-

meter sprint. Her weaknesses were the shot put, javelin, and 800-meter run. Thus, her coach and husband, Bob, worked specifically to strengthen those three areas. The world championships in Rome were coming up. This would be the last international meet before the Olympics, so it was important that Jackie do well.

Plus, she had another goal: breaking 7200 points.

Impossible? She'd already scored over 7100 twice. That proved her high scores weren't flukes. She felt better than ever, even though she suffered from asthma, a breathing disorder, and various athletic problems like pulled tendons and ligaments and twisted knees. She trained with world-record intensity, totally dedicating herself to her sport. Plus, she wanted another record. Yes, the 7200-point mark was definitely possible.

In the meantime, she captured gold medals in a number of smaller contests, the most significant of which was the Pan American Games in Indianapolis, just two weeks before the world championships. Remember, Jackie was not only a heptathlete; she was also an outstanding long jumper. The long jump was an event she cherished, as it was the first she ever competed in, at age fourteen. Holding a world record in that event would be the cherry on top of the chocolate sundae. Thus, against her coach-husband's advice, she went to the Pan American Games.

The world record in the long jump, 24 feet, 5 1/2 inches, was held by an East German named Heike Drechsler. One day a fan asked Jackie to sign a picture of herself in a magazine. Next to her picture was one of Heike in mid-flight. Jackie noticed how Heike's feet extended out in front of her when she long-jumped. Bob had long encouraged her to try this tactic.

So at the Pan Am Games, Jackie added it to her kit of surprises. She raced down the track, leaped, extended her legs, and seemed to never come down. Measuring the jump, the judges instantly realized they had witnessed something remarkable. Jackie had tied the world record. She became the first and only American woman ever to hold world records in a single event and a multi-event at the same time! Her husband, witnessing the jump, fell to his knees in joy and praise, crying. Not just because she'd won, but because he had almost kept her from coming to the Games.

They went on to the World Championships in Rome at the end of August. There, Jackie logged another stellar performance, winning the gold with 7,129 points and beating second place by over 500 points. However, she didn't crack the 7200 ceiling.

She was disappointed, but then she realized she possessed the three highest-scoring heptathlons in history. That cheered her up for a moment.

Soon it would be on to the 1988 Olympics. Jackie had dreamed of that moment since she was a gangly fourteen-year-old back in East St. Louis. She had already set numerous records and was considered the best athlete in America. She had a silver medal from the 1984 Olympics and numerous golds from other important competitions. And she claimed the top three scores ever recorded in the heptathlon, as well as a tie for the world record in the long jump.

What more could she want?

Two things: an Olympic gold medal, and to break 7200 points.

Could it be done? Many athletes and observers said no. Not even someone as talented and committed as Jackie Joyner-Kersee could break that barrier, even though it was likely she would win the gold.

Before that, though, some rest was needed.

And there were other things—like a community center in East St. Louis for disadvantaged kids. And speaking to various groups. And giving her testimony in churches.

So Jackie was still busy.

The first step was the Olympic Trials in Indianapolis. Already, someone else besides Jackie was making waves with her style and her record-breaking. That was Florence Griffith-Joyner, wife of Jackie's brother Al. She had burned up the track in the 100 meters, 200 meters, and the 4 X 100-meter relay. Suddenly, it looked like the two sisters-in-law would dominate.

And dominate they did. Florence took firsts in all her events. Jackie, meanwhile, turned her attention to the long jump and the heptathlon.

The first day of the heptathlon competition, Jackie broke three American records: the 100-meter hurdles, the 200-meter sprint, and the high jump. The next day she logged the same kind of results. At the end, Jackie was 969 points ahead of the second-place finisher, Cindy Greiner. And she had demolished the 7200 barrier with 7,215 points.

Now for the Seoul, South Korea 1988 Olympics, Jackie had a new goal : 7300 points. She now held the top four heptathlon marks of all time. She also had long-jumped 24 feet, 5 inches, just a half inch shorter than her own world record. It looked like Seoul would be the icing on a very large, tasty cake.

The sunny, beautiful Olympic day started wonderfully warm and happy for Jackie. She ran 12.69 seconds in the 100-meter hurdles, an Olympic best. (In the heptathlon, records can only be tallied after all seven events are done. So within individual events, high marks are labeled "bests" rather than records.)

But then in the high jump, Jackie planted her left foot for the leap slightly off base and twisted her knee. It looked like a disaster. She only jumped 6 feet, 1 1/4 inches, over two inches under her best of

6 feet, 4 inches. It was almost the same injury that had dogged her at the 1984 Olympics. Would she have to settle for a silver? Or worse, no medal at all?

Jackie did what she always does in such circumstances. She got tough on herself, prayed, and decided to ignore the pain.

She moved on to the shot put and posted a throw of 15.8 meters, almost as far as her personal best. Then she won the last event of the day, the 200-meter sprint, in 22.56 seconds.

It appeared that the twisted knee wasn't so much of a problem after all. She was only slightly behind world-record pace.

The next day, though, she would face two of her toughest events—the javelin and the 800-meter run. Could she do it?

Her doctor examined her that afternoon and discovered she had strained a tendon in her knee. Such a tendon, under more stress, could rupture or tear. It was a dangerous condition. The therapist treated her, but Jackie was not about to drop out of the competition.

The next morning, Jackie walked out onto the field, shaky but ready. Her best event, the long jump, was next. She hoped to make only one jump, although she was allowed three. She wanted to rest that knee for the javelin and the run.

She leaped 23 feet, 10 1/4 inches, off from her best of 24 feet, 5 1/2 inches, but good enough for an Olympic heptathlon best. She was on her way.

The javelin, she knew, would be more difficult. She normally pushed off with her left foot, and that injured knee might not hold. As she threw, she felt pain in the knee. It was close to tearing. Her best effort in the javelin was 149 feet, 10 inches, over ten feet less than her career best.

Could she still win? And what about that record?

She went into the 800 meters with grit teeth. She asked her husband-coach, "What do I need?" That is, what time do I need to break the record? His answer was, 2:13.67.

Jackie said, "If I can't run that, if I can't give the people a world record, I don't deserve to be here."[1]

She needed a fast start and determination to bring home the gold. And the record. She didn't have to actually win the race, though, just beat the time her husband had quoted.

She ran like lightning. As the pain cranked up, she scolded herself, "Block it out. If your legs aren't burning, you can still run." As she reached the backstretch of the last lap, with a little more than half a lap to go, three East Germans plugged on ahead of her and began to pull away. When she hit the finish line, she was in fifth place. But she needed to see the time.

It was 2:08.51.

A new world record for the heptathlon—7,291 points.

And a gold medal.

Jackie had come a long way. From a poverty-stricken upbringing, to UCLA on a scholarship, to an

Olympic gold medal and world record. She had made her mark, and it is a mark that has stayed.

But that wasn't the end of it!

There was still the long jump. And a Russian and an East German to beat. Five days after the heptathlon, she went jump for jump with the best, including her old rival, Heike Drechsler. The Russian, Galina Chistyakova, started off with a jump of 23 feet, 4 inches. Then Heike chimed in with 23 feet, 8 1/4 inches. Jackie struck a median point with 23 feet, 6 inches. She would have to do better than that.

Through four rounds, the finalists remained in that order: Galina third, Jackie second, and Heike first.

Then came the fifth round. Jackie had faulted on the two previous jumps, so it was getting down to the wire. But this time, as 50,000 people looked on in the stadium, Jackie bounded down the track, leaped, and soared 24 feet, 3 1/2 inches. A new Olympic record.

No one caught her. Jackie took home the gold in the long jump too.

Two gold medals. The greatest athlete in the world. And a Christian to boot.

Not a bad combination.

---

1. Neil Cohen, "Jackie Joyner-Kersee," *Sports Illustrated for Kids Book* (Boston: Little, Brown, and Company, 1992), 5–6.

Chapter 4

©Allsport

☆ Brian Diemer ☆

Height: 5 feet, 9 1/2 inches

Weight: 142 pounds

Born: October 10, 1961

Sport: Track and field

Years in Olympics: 1984, 1988, 1992, 1996

Brian Diemer: Smallest Guy on the Block

Smallest guy on the block. In the class. On the team. Someone has to be the smallest guy. And many of those who are, decide early on that there's no point in trying to be the best. They just aren't big enough.

For Brian Diemer, being smallest meant one thing: try harder.

And try harder he did. As a kid he loved all sports—baseball, football, basketball, track. He made the teams by giving 100 percent and more. For him, size was only part of the equation. Finesse, talent, commitment, determination—those were the things that counted.

They could help you win! Even against all odds.

Brian grew up in Cutlerville, Michigan, a town outside of Grand Rapids. He lived on a farm with parents who didn't farm. His father worked in the landscaping business and often used the farm and the family to practice. Brian had one younger brother and two sisters, one younger than he and one older.

In the tenth grade, Brian developed an interest in running as a means to get into better shape for basketball. But Brian discovered he had a special ability in running, especially in the area of endurance. Long distances pleased him. He could deal with the pain, and he enjoyed the feeling of running at length.

Eventually, running replaced basketball because Brian wanted to run all winter. He ran track and cross-country beginning in tenth grade and, in the fall of 1978, won the state cross-country championship. He was small, but he was number one. He also won the state mile run in 1978 and 1979, recording a best time of 4:14, not bad for a high schooler, and certainly something to be proud of. In addition, he excelled in the two-mile race and won the state championship in 1979 with a time of 9:22.

The coach at the University of Michigan recruited Brian and gave him a scholarship. He was supposed to run the mile and two mile. But one day during his freshman year, the coach made a few of the long-distance guys jump over a steeplechase water pit, simply to see if any of them could do it. The team needed personnel for the event, but no one had expressed interest. The coach decided to motivate interest by getting some of the guys into the act.

The steeplechase is a 3000-meter event, just under two miles. Runners go around the track seven times, jumping over five barriers per lap along the way—four dry barriers and one wet barrier. Each dry barrier is three feet high and looks like a big sawhorse, or a wide hurdle. In fact, the steeplechase is a little like the hurdles, but with three differences. One, the barriers are farther apart. Two, there are thirty-five of them in a race, not ten. And three, they're fixed on the ground. If a runner strikes one with a leg, the barrier doesn't fall down—the runner does.

The wet barrier, called the water pit, is three feet high and twelve feet wide, the top being made of a long piece of six-by-six-inch timber. The pit behind the barrier is filled with water and stretches out for twelve feet; the water is two and a half feet deep next to the barrier and gradually shallows until it meets the track at the twelve-foot mark. So the runners jump up onto the top of the barrier and leap. Most of the time, they make the twelve feet and avoid the water. However, as the race goes on, many runners get tired and land in the water. It cools them off, but it doesn't win races.

When as a freshman Brian first saw this monstrosity that day, he was intrigued. Could he make it all the way over? Could he do it seven times in a complete race? Could he do it well enough to win?

The coach sent the guys running down toward the barrier. Brian jumped up to the top and leaped—and came down on his foot just on the other side of the water! He'd made it!

When he looked back, he saw some of the others plowing through the water. They hadn't leaped far enough.

Afterward, the coach said, "You're going to try it in the next race."

He did, and he ran well. A steeplechaser was born.

Not many people notice or think about the steeplechase. When we consider track events, we think of the 100-meter dash or the 400 meters or the half mile or mile. But the steeplechase?

Though it doesn't get the press in our country, in many other places in the world it's a revered event. Steeplechasers are heroes. They run a grueling, painful race in which they have to leap thirty-five times, more than any of the hurdle races. By the sixth or seventh lap, they're exhausted. Those barriers look like mountains, and that water pit just like a swimming pool. Why not plunk down and breathe easy?

But they have to go on! It's a race, the steeple-chase. And there are guys coming from behind, chasing you to the next steeple!

Brian discovered that he loved this event, and he devoted himself to it exclusively. The steeplechase, like all long-distance races, requires strategic think-ing and tactical brilliance. The runners cannot expend themselves too early, or they will have no energy left for the final stretch. Nor can they give every leap a maximum effort and so wear them-selves down. Each runner must think of ways to con-serve energy and still remain a contender. That often means running with the pack and laying back behind the leaders.

Running with the pack, though, is dangerous in the steeplechase. Runners don't run in lanes, so everyone is bunched up. A participant can easily hurt an ankle, or trip, or smack the back of someone's leg and get thrown off course. At each leap, a runner might get belted in the lips by the flailing arms of a neighboring runner.

So a runner has to be careful. Wise as a serpent and innocent as a dove, as the Bible says. That's good strategy for a steeplechaser.

Runners tend to go fast and slow, fast and slow. Brian thinks of it as kind of like a slinky—fast as it runs between barriers, and then slow when it hits the bar-riers. The constantly changing pace makes the event even harder. Participants are always starting up and then slowing down, sometimes coming to a complete stop when they jump over the water pit. Good steeple-chasers try not to slow down over the barriers.

Brian went on to excel in the steeplechase and to win. By his senior year he was winning all his races. In the NCAA Division I championships in 1983, Brian looked forward to racing against the best steeple-chasers in the United States.

In fact, it was in the NCAAs that Brian started dreaming of something he'd never given much thought to before: the Olympics. Prior to the NCAA meet, Brian knew he was a good steeplechaser, but he certainly didn't think he was the best. To get into the Olympics, he'd have to be one of the top three in the country, and he wasn't sure he was that good. So when he entered the NCAAs, he planned on hanging up his spikes afterward and getting on with the rest of his life.

Then he won the race with a time of 8:26. Suddenly, all his plans changed. He had qualified to go to the U.S. nationals. He went to that meet wondering if he really had the ability to be one of the best. There he finished second with a time of 8:22.

The top three from the nationals went on to Helsinki, Finland, for the World Championships. There, Brian came in thirteenth. He knew that in the Olympics he had to finish in the top twelve to make it to the finals. And for the first time, he thought he might make it. He was fired up now to make the Olympic team.

Ron Warhurst, Brian's coach at Michigan, had coached such stars as Greg Meyer, who won the Boston Marathon in 1983, and Bill and Gerard Donakowski, who were both tremendous 5000- and 10,000-meter runners. Ron encouraged Brian to go all the way.

Together, they trained hard and Brian came in second at the U.S. Olympic Trials with an 8:17. Henry Marsh from Salt Lake City won first, running about two seconds faster.

Brian had made the Olympics. He was going to race in the big time!

Because the United States boycotted the Moscow Olympics in 1980, the Russians and other communist countries boycotted the 1984 Olympics in Los Angeles. That eliminated a runner from Poland who might have been in medal contention. But despite the boycott, Brian was thrilled to be running on an Olympic team. It was the fulfillment of a major dream. Until the year before, he had never thought it was possible. But after winning the nationals and going to the World Championships, Brian felt the dream become really intense.

What was it like to run in the Olympics?

Brian says, "Walking into the stadium and hearing 90,000 people cheering and screaming was tremendous. We all paraded into the stadium in our uniforms, nation by nation, and the place just erupted when the Americans walked in. It was the most incredible feeling. Suddenly, I realized there were millions, maybe billions of people watching around the world. I got real nervous thinking about that. But I focused my mind and got into gear about the competition coming up."

Brian wanted to do his best, of course. And he hoped to actually win a medal. It was an adrenaline-pumping time.

The steeplechase competition was held on August 8, 10, and 12, during the second week of the Olympics. About forty of the best steeplechasers in the world ran in the initial heats. That would be cut down to twenty-four for the semifinals and then to twelve for the finals.

Brian felt good in his heat. "It was actually a cakewalk, because it only took 8:30 to qualify. I was sure I could run that. I'd done it plenty of times before. Still, it was the survival of the fittest. I had to be in the top five in my heat to advance." Which is exactly what he did. He made it to the semis.

Now Brian knew he'd have to work harder—only six of the twelve semifinalists would qualify for the finals. Brian ran well, conserving his energy and finishing strong in 8:18. He didn't wear himself out and appeared to be on target for an even better time in the next race.

In the finals, Brian knew he had to place in the top three to medal. His primary contenders were the American who had beaten him in the Olympic Trials, Henry Marsh, and Julius Korir from Kenya. It would be a tough run.

The race was tight the whole way. Brian remained in the back of the pack for a while, but then slowly worked his way up. With three laps to go, he reached the front, leaping the barriers with finesse. The crowd, mostly American, roared its approval, excited to see one of their own in contention so late in the race.

On the last lap, Korir took off. Brian remained in fourth place until the last thirty yards, when he passed Henry Marsh for third place. Joseph Mamoud from France took the silver. Brian had run 8:14, one of his best times ever. He had the bronze medal.

"It didn't hit me right away, what I had really done, until I walked on out to the podium and my family came down to the railing. They were all crying and happy and excited. I watched the American flag go up. It was a tremendous joy."

Brian has competed in two other Olympics, in 1988, where he finished fifteenth with an 8:23, and in 1992, where he finished seventh with an 8:18. He plans to try out for the Olympic team again this coming year. In the meantime, he works as head cross-country coach and distance coach in track at Calvin College in Grand Rapids, Michigan.

For Brian though, there were two other great moments in his life that may rank above the Olympics.

The first was becoming a Christian.

He grew up in a Christian home, and went to church and a Christian school all his life. "I never really made a real commitment to the Lord until the summer before I went to the University of Michigan. I knew it was time for me to choose which way I wanted to go. I went to the freshman orientation there and found myself being offered everything you can imagine—alcohol, drugs, sex. I determined then and there to commit my life to the Lord.

"The Spirit had been working in me for quite a long time. I had started up my own private devotions. I was greatly challenged all the time at school after I made the commitment. A lot of people teased me when I prayed before my meals. But that was gratifying, because the people that teased me, later began to respect me. I received some letters and things from people who were encouraged by the fact that I prayed before my meals and was not swayed by the people around me."

Brian doesn't see his running as an end in itself. For him it's a means to further God's kingdom. "He's given me the talent to run, which is wonderful. But more importantly He's given me a platform to spread His Word. Being involved in sports gives me many great opportunities to witness."

That brings us to that other high point. It happened through his relationship with a young man from Czechoslovakia.

"In 1983 I had one fall semester left in college. I went over to Czechoslovakia on a Christian track team. We had to raise three thousand dollars to be part of it, and we went to various countries. Track was our platform and we'd give testimonies.

"The great thing was, I made friends with a kid over there—Tomas Kosmak. He was a 5000-meter runner. I ran in a race in Prague, and afterwards, he stopped and talked to me. He could speak English, so we struck up a friendship. He and I talked many times about my faith. When I left the country, we corresponded for many years after that. I sent him a Bible and various verses in letters.

"In 1989, he and his wife were able to purchase a trip down to Greece with his family (one son). While they truly wanted to take a vacation there, they had something else planned too. They had to have so much money before they could even apply to take a trip. They had saved for years. At the time, they weren't even thinking about going on a trip. The

61

day that a special group tour package was offered, Tomas just happened to walk past the travel agent and decided to stop. He bought the package. I believe now it was God's leading.

"The family went on down to Greece. They waited for the right moment, then left their group and went to the U.S. embassy in Athens. They wanted to defect. They were in Athens for two years and we helped support them with money and clothing. Finally, after much work and negotiation, they were accepted into the U.S. They flew here to Grand Rapids, and we helped them start life in the U.S. He's a painter and has started a new venture with a builder.

"Today he and his wife and three kids live in the Grand Rapids area. They have become very committed Christians. In a church just two weeks ago, he and I gave the story how all that happened. He gives God the credit for how things worked out so perfectly in his life. He can see how everything was orchestrated."

Helping Tomas, also an athlete, has been a real highlight for Brian, perhaps more so even than the Olympics. For him, giving, serving, loving, and helping are what being a Christian is all about.

"I can see God working in me from the time I was the smallest kid in the class. He had a lot of things in store for me. The running was not an end in itself, but a means. God has used me in so many different ways that all I can say is that it's for His glory."

What advice would Brian give a prospective steeplechaser? "If you're trying to get better at running, run every day. Don't let little things get in the way and ruin your focus. And consistently be in the Word of God."

Brian's still running for the kingdom and for God. And even if he's not so small anymore, he gives God all the glory. Brian says that God can use you—big or small—and He'll use you in a way that you'll love!

For Brian Diemer, that isn't just the main thing, it's the only thing.

☆ Madeline Manning Mims ☆

Height: 5 feet, 9 inches

Weight: 135 pounds

Birth date: January 11, 1948

Sport: Track and field

Years in Olympics: 1968, 1972, 1976

Madeline Manning Mims: God's Ambassador

- Member of four Olympic teams
- Olympic medalist
- First American woman to break two minutes in the 800 meters
- Ranked number one amateur athlete in the world in her event, 1967, 1968, and 1969
- National outdoor champion eight times

- National indoor champion six times
- Four times Olympic Trials champion
- Olympic women's track team captain three times
- Holder of American outdoor record for the women's 800 meters for fifteen years (best time: 1:57.9)

The list could go on, but let's stop there and take a breath.

Wow! What an athlete!

But who is this champion, Christian, speaker, and singer named Madeline Manning Mims?

Madeline was born in the ghetto of Cleveland, Ohio, in 1948. Her father drank himself out of his home and out of his marriage. Madeline's mother worked hard, though, and kept the family together.

At age three, Madeline suffered from a near-fatal bout of spinal meningitis, a children's disease that often kills or cripples its victims. The doctors told her mother that she had only a fifty-fifty chance of surviving, and that if she did she'd be mentally retarded. She'd never be physically able to do the things most other kids could do.

Madeline's mom wasn't dismayed, though. She went right to her knees and prayed passionately and daily for the survival of her daughter. God heard her, and Madeline came through. She remained a sickly girl until her teens, but she had a driving ambition to succeed. She wasn't physically or mentally handicapped after all. In fact, just the reverse. She excelled while others fell behind.

At age six, Madeline made her commitment to Jesus Christ. Her Sunday school teacher gave her a little card with a picture of Jesus the Good Shepherd. The picture featured Jesus holding a little black lamb. At that moment, Madeline suddenly saw herself in Jesus' arms. She says today, "It's the only time I've ever seen that kind of picture." It communicated to her the Savior's love, grace, and commitment to all people, regardless of color or race.

She walked up to the teacher and pointed to the picture. "Who's that?" she asked.

"That's Jesus," the teacher said. "He protects little lambs."

Madeline said, "Can he hold me like that?"

"Yes, of course."

So Madeline closed her eyes tightly and said, "I'm ready."

She and the teacher knelt down and prayed. Suddenly a warm, accepting feeling rushed all through her body. After the prayer, she smiled, opened her eyes widely, and said to the teacher, "He's got me."

And He's had her ever since. That commitment has remained in force through all her later years of glory and racing. She never forgot who got her that day and who would hold her ever after.

While in elementary school in Cleveland, Madeline won nearly every medal and ribbon possible in track. She was discovered through the Presidential Physical Fitness test, sponsored by President John F. Kennedy's administration. She did well on the tests in high school, but when another classmate scored better Madeline decided to go back and take the same tests over again. This time she set some new standards nationally.

In high school, Madeline competed on the volleyball, basketball, and track teams. From the tenth to the twelfth grade her school won the state championships in all three sports. But track is where Madeline would make her mark.

Madeline ran the 440-yard dash, the 220, and the 4 X 100 relay. The first time she ran in the 440 she set a new school record—59.0 seconds. (The 800 meters wasn't really known in her part of the country.) At the state championships, she finished well ahead of the field in the 440 and was the first girl in the world to run it in 55 seconds. That was where her first coach, Alex Ferenczy, noticed her.

Mr. Ferenczy worked Madeline very hard. "He'd work me so hard, there were times when I thought he was trying to kill me, but it paid off. His coaching genius was a gift from God."

Ferenczy saw her potential and realized she could go all the way. When she was in tenth grade she made the American National Women's Track and Field team and represented the United States in Russia, West Germany, and Poland.

Madeline's original interest in the 800 meters event occurred through a curious circumstance. It happened like this: In the eleventh grade she went to Toronto, Canada, to run the 400 meters in the Maple Leaf Games, an indoor event. However, most of the girls who entered the 400 were really half milers, and they wanted to change the race from the 400- to the 800-meter run, the metric equivalent of the half mile. While Madeline went to the bathroom, the officials called for a vote. When Madeline came back, she discovered the race had been changed from 400 meters to 800 meters. Madeline says today, "Never go to the bathroom until they've decided what you're going to run."

Her coach told her to use the 800 as a practice run and to follow whoever was out front leading. "I didn't know he was psyching me. I had never run where you didn't have your own lane. The official told us we would run it on the waterline. That means that you curve in and everyone is next to each other, fighting for position in the same lane.

At the gun, the field just took off. The inside lane suddenly opened up and Madeline shot through.

"By the time we got to the other side of the track," says Madeline, "I was leading. So I started to slow it down. Then a girl from Yugoslavia came around and took the lead. I just started following after her. I mean, this was only practice for me, right?

"Then, with a littler over a lap to go, her coach shouted out to the Yugoslav girl in English, 'Leave her, she's getting tired.' He thought I was getting tired. But I wasn't, so I took his advice and began to leave *her*. I forgot completely what I'd already run—it was like I was just starting out—and I went into another phase of running mentally. I really started to pour it on. I was speeding around that last lap, sprinting. I won by a little less than a half lap. I'd never run a half mile before."

She ended up with a women's indoor world record, 2:10.2. As an eleventh grader! Madeline had captured a great world record. "My plan at the time was to run the 200 and the 400. But now that I had the world record in the 800, everybody wanted me to run the half. After Toronto, most of the meets I was invited to, I would run both the 400 and the 800."

The next year, Madeline won a scholarship to Tennessee State University. The coach, Mr. Edward Temple, brought her in as an 800/400 runner.

Her first year there, 1967, the Pan American Games were scheduled in Canada. By this time, Madeline was rated number one in the world in the half mile. She'd won many races, and this seemed like just one more. At the Pan American Games, as expected, she won a gold medal and set a new American record. She had entered a period when she would hold the national record for fifteen years. And this was only the beginning.

The Olympics were coming in 1968 to Mexico City, and an excitement filled Madeline's heart, and that of her praying mom. No one had expected Madeline to go this far, especially when she had been so sickly as a child. But now her name was up in lights and she occupied the place of a champion.

Madeline was the favorite to win the 800 at Mexico City. "It was kind of funny," Madeline says now. "When everything was over, Jim McKay, the sportscaster, made this big statement on TV. He kept calling me a big surprise, even though for the last two years I'd been the top half miler in the world. It was like he didn't know what he was talking about. But I didn't let it bother me. It was all part of the times."

Madeline was actually something of a pioneer in women's track. African American women, in particular, were regarded as sprinters—the 100 meters and 200 meters, races like that. No African American had broken into the longer distances. Madeline received a lot of ignorant hate mail from people who wanted her to move over and let a white girl win.

"I had dealt with prejudice before running the 800. People didn't like me taking the awards away from the white girls. I didn't have as much trouble with it as my coach did."

Madeline's high school coach, Alex Ferenczy, was the women's Olympic coach. He was Hungarian, and tended to get emotional. He'd say things like, "One day they're going to beg for you to come back here, and when they do, I'm going to say no."

The Olympics took Madeline a step further in her faith as well, not only because she'd been receiving this hate mail, but also because she realized God was with her in a special way. She prayed, "God, You gave me this talent. I've done everything I know to do with it. No one knows what will happen in the Olympics but You. So I'm going to run for Your glory."

She won her heat, then her semifinal, and then the finals. Her time in the 800 was 2:00.87, an Olympic, American, and world record. She found herself standing on the winner's platform with a gold medal around her neck.

"Going through competition is like dying," she says now. "There's so much pressure that it feels like the butterflies in your stomach are turning into wasps and stinging the walls of your stomach.

"But when I stood on that winner's pedestal, and they played the National Anthem, my life flashed before me. I looked up at the flag in amazement. Wow, that's flying because of me."[1]

After the ceremonies, Jim McKay brought Madeline before the television cameras and asked her, "Who do you give the glory to for getting you to this point?"

Madeline says, "I'm sure he was looking for a different answer. But I said, 'I give all the glory to God. I'm running for Jesus.'

"He said, 'We're not talking religion here.'

"I said, 'Neither am I.' It was the first time any athlete had openly shared their faith on TV. It was an honest answer.

"He then said, 'We'll return to track and field after these messages.' A commercial came on!

"It was an awesome moment in time, and I knew something special had happened."

Out of that event comes a wonderful story of God's work in others through Madeline's witness.

This is what happened: In a previous Europe versus America Games Madeline had competed against an excellent runner, Vera Nikolic, from Yugoslavia. In the semifinals at Mexico City, Madeline ran against her for the first time in an Olympics. At the end of the run, she turned around to see who were the first four finishers who would run in the finals. Madeline expected to see Vera, but couldn't find her.

"I asked several competitors where she was, and I found out she had only run about three hundred meters, then stopped and walked off the track. I knew she would be my heaviest opponent, so something was wrong."

Madeline later found out that Vera had been pressured by her country's diplomats to come home with nothing less than a gold medal.

"She had walked out of the stadium," Madeline says, "walked onto a bridge, and tried to jump off. Her coach caught her and stopped her in time, but she was emotionally crushed and broken.

"Just before the finals, I saw Vera. I had never seen anyone so void of hope. I wanted to go to her and talk, but everyone was heading over to the stadium for the finals. Still, I had enough time, and I told my teammate to tell my coach I would catch the next bus.

"I walked back toward Vera. Two people were standing by her. I kept calling her, but she wouldn't answer. Finally, I grabbed her shoulders and held her. She had such emptiness in her eyes. It was the first time I'd ever seen eyes like that. I tried to talk to her. She spoke very little English. I spoke no Yugoslavian.

"There was no response. I finally said, 'I don't know if you understand me or not, but I want you to know God created you an athlete. Go home and put this all behind you. You need to find your relationship with God. When you find that, everything will be all right. You're young. You can put this behind you. God is on your side.'

"She cried. I embraced her. We both stood there crying. I walked off and ran my race."

At the next year's Europe versus America Games, Vera's coach told Madeline that Vera had just started running again. He said, "We left Mexico City and they put her in a mental institution. She wouldn't talk. I went to visit her at one point and finally she started talking and said, 'Madeline came back. She was on her way to her finals and she came back just to talk to me.'"

Madeline says now, with the hint of a tear in her eye, "Those words told me why I was born. It gave me the purpose for which I was created. I wasn't born just to win gold medals. I was given life so I could give it away to someone else who was dying."

After the coach explained Vera's situation to Madeline, she suddenly turned around and there was Vera, shouting Madeline's name. She said, "I found God. I found God, Madeline."

That's not the end of the story, though.

Madeline made the team for the 1972 Olympics in Munich, Germany. But, unfortunately, in an early heat, an official misdirected the whole field as to where the finish line was. In effect, the official told the contestants to stop at the wrong place. At the end of the race, Madeline reached the line and stopped, as did the three runners ahead of her. No one told them they hadn't finished the race. As later finishers arrived, it was a real horror show. Everyone leaped for the real finish line at once.

It took the officials fifteen minutes to figure out who had qualified for the finals. When the results came in, Madeline was edged out of fourth place by two centimeters. She was out of the Olympic 800 meters.

Madeline says with a smile, "I was sitting in the stadium tunnel, and my friend Vera stayed with me. She was very sorry for me. But then she said, 'You're young. You can put this behind you. And anyway, you have God on your side.'

"I was stunned. It was the same thing I'd told her four years ago."

Following the Olympics, Madeline broke the two-minute barrier in the 800 meters in 1976, at a meet in Maryland against the Russians. Her time of 1:57.9 set another American record for her, a record she had held for over nine years already, and would hold for six more.

Today, Madeline works for her own company, called Ambassadorship, Inc. An ordained Protestant minister, she frequently serves as an athlete chaplain at various games. She sings, speaks, and talks to young people. But her main priority is ministering to athletes. She prays with them, spiritually prepares them to compete, and does one-on-one counseling through building long-term relationships.

What advice might she give to young people hoping to run competitively and possibly make it to an Olympics?

"Look for the gift God has given you and use it. Develop your gifts. They will make you successful in life. You're just now developing your skills and your character. Don't try to judge who you are by someone else."

And above all, run for Jesus and His glory.

---

1. "Madeline Mims: God's Ambassador," *Triumphant Always*, premier issue, 1995, 17.

★ Josh Davis ★

Chapter 6

Height: 6 feet, 2 1/2 inches

Weight: 185 pounds

Birth date: September 1, 1972

Sport: Swimming

Years in Olympics: 1996

©Allsport

Josh Davis: Like a Dolphin

Remember the last time you went swimming? Gliding through the water? Diving? Blowing spray into the wind?

How fast are you?

If speed is what you're looking for, then take a look at Josh Davis. He happens to be one of the speediest swimmers in the world.

When he was about twelve, Josh and his family moved into a new neighborhood. His new friends were all swimmers, so the family enrolled Josh on the country-club team. He spent the next few years winning third- and fourth-place ribbons. He wanted to get some firsts, so he decided to swim year-round.

In ninth grade, Josh was a tall, skinny kid with few muscles and no swimming technique, and his coach didn't think he would make varsity.

There's a lesson in that. When you believe in yourself but your coach doesn't, it's time to switch coaches, not necessarily switch sports. So Josh found a new coach to work with—a man named Jim Yates.

With Yates's help, Josh went straight to the varsity. Coach Yates took the time to teach Josh the principles found in all the great swim books. While anybody can read a book, a true coach helps his swimmer develop technique. Coach Yates answered Josh's questions and showed him what to do. He worked with Josh on a daily basis, critiquing the young swimmer and helping him improve his speed.

Freestyle soon emerged as Josh's best stroke.

Josh says, "Swimming is a sport of habit, learning to do the same stroke over and over. You do a stroke in the right way, your muscles learn a good habit, and vice versa. Coach stuck with me to help me learn the right habits. As I got older, stronger, more fit, I became very successful. Coach just believed I had potential."

Physiologically speaking, Josh had several attributes that the coach recognized: big hands and feet; long arms; a slender, angular frame; and a good "feel" for the water. What is that "feel"?

"It's a gift to understand how your body moves through water. It can come with training, but some people learn it naturally. I was one of those who just had it, like it was a gift of God. Of course, I didn't think of it that way then. But that was coming."

Swimming is a big-time event in Texas. The state finals are one of the most exciting swim meets in the nation. Swimmers go through the city finals, then the regional finals, and finally, they reach the state finals. In a large state like Texas, hordes of contestants are involved.

As a tenth grader, Josh won state in the 200-yard freestyle and also swam second leg on his school's championship 4 X 100-yard freestyle relay team.

At the end of that season, Coach Yates gathered the team together and challenged them to crack the national high school record of 3:02.61 in the 4 X 100-yard free relay. He said, "I want you to hang onto this and make it your goal to break it."

After that, Josh thought nothing but 3:02.61. Break it. Knock it to pieces. Swimming as fast as a porpoise, gliding through the water super-fast, like a dolphin, he—and his team members—felt an excitement.

"I was learning an important lesson about sports at the time. That lesson is to set goals and be specific. It was a turning point for me. It introduced me to the importance of goal setting, positive thinking, being specific—all those things. It made me hunger to do something."

His junior year he swam better than ever. He was growing physically, his body becoming long, sleek, and angular, perfect for racing through the water at high speeds. He was ready to assault the relay record, and ready to defend his state title in the 200-yard freestyle.

That year, 1989, he repeated as 200-yard freestyle champion. He doesn't recall the exact time, but it was about a 1:40.

And then there was the relay. The crowd roared for a record-breaking time. Everyone watched Josh's team. They were the favorites, the team everyone wanted to beat.

The eight teams lined up. Bang! Off they went, off the blocks and into the smooth water. Josh felt a power in and around him as he swam. It was marvelous. When the team finished in first place, they immediately turned to the clock. It read 3:02.41. They had broken the record by two-tenths of a second!

That record still stands today.

Josh's senior year, his team again won the 4 X 100-yard relay. He didn't win the 200-yard freestyle, but he had posted a state-record time of 1:36.5 earlier in the year.

It was time to look at colleges and decide which to attend. It had to be a school where swimming played an important role. The best swimming schools in the country were the University of Texas at Austin—they had won three national championships in the last three years—Stanford University, and the University of Michigan. Josh could have had a full scholarship to any school he wanted, but it came down to Stanford and UT.

"I chose Texas over Stanford. Ed Reese, the coach there, was the best coach for me. I didn't want to fly off to California without getting all I could out of Texas anyway. That was where I grew up. UT was far enough away for me to get away from home, but close enough so my family could come and watch me swim. At the time, UT had won three national NCAA championships, Division I."

Josh headed off to UT.

He was excited to be at the university, and his freshman year was excellent. Josh felt like a kid in a candy store. He wanted to make great grades, meet all the girls he could, party, and have fun.

Josh's life in the fast lane was put on hold until after his team won the national championship. Josh

 had been one of the top freshman on the team, a major point contributor. He participated on two winning relays, 4 X 100-yard and 4 X 200-yard freestyle, and

83

finished in the final eight in the 100- and 200-yard freestyle.

Josh remembers that 100-yard freestyle especially. "It was the most exciting race of the meet. There were seven seniors in the final and I was the only freshman. I was between two guys from USC [University of Southern California]. One was six-ten and the other was six-seven. I felt like a dwarf.

"Also in the heat were several former Olympians and national champions. Shaun Jordan, a gold medal winner, swam the 4 X 100-meter relay in the 1988 and 1992 Olympics. Jon Olsen was also on the 1992 relays that won the gold medals."

Josh was awed. "They were the country's top freestylers in the last half-decade, and I was in the heat with them!"

Josh didn't choke as he thought he might. His seventh-place finish is misleading, because his time was a mere second and a half behind the winner. "I swam a 43.9. Shaun Jordan was number one with a 42.4."

After returning from winning the national championship, he started going out again, partying very hard. He had just gotten a new girlfriend. Also, the pressures of school picked up with final examinations. Life in the fast lane was wearing on him. After finals he became very ill.

"My mom picked me up from school. I went home to San Antonio and laid in bed for two weeks.

I did a lot of thinking. God had brought me to the bottom of the barrel, and all I could do was look up."

Josh felt he needed a new direction. "I pulled out an old prayer book I had as a kid that was stuffed into my shelves at home. I found some things an Athletes in Action member had given me. I began to pray a simple prayer, admitting to God that I didn't know what I was doing. I wanted Him to take control and make me the kind of man He wanted me to be. I guess God gave me enough strength and courage to respond to His truth."

His conversion happened that summer.

"Christians I knew showed me love and acceptance: my friends from Athletes in Action (AIA) and FCA (Fellowship of Christian Athletes), friends in other sports that I hung around with. The distinction between me and my old friends was immense. I knew I couldn't live like I had been back at school. And I wondered what would happen."

When he arrived back at school in the fall, everyone expected Josh to lead the way in a party lifestyle. But Josh's new relationship with Jesus Christ prevented him from doing that.

"It was a character-building year. My friends didn't understand what God had done in my heart. Some took offense, like it was a personal attack. I started building many more friendships with strong Christians. I realized early on the importance of Christian fellowship.

"I was fortunate that I had several older men disciple me and pour into my life: one from my church in Austin (Hyde Park Baptist), a man from AIA. And another who was willing to spend time with me and counsel me."

Josh grew and held onto his faith like a lineman holding a fumbled football. He knew he played for a new team now and things would change. Though the guys on the swim team didn't immediately accept Josh's new faith, they didn't put him down either. As they saw him perform in the pool, they knew he was basically the same athlete. The "killer's edge" had not slackened, even if he did say "Praise the Lord" now and then.

Josh lived differently during his sophomore year, which put some strain on relationships. He began to learn what it means to be a Christian athlete, what kind of standards he had to meet. In the pool, Josh's team was shooting for a fifth consecutive NCAA championship. Individually, Josh competed at the Olympic Trials.

"It's extremely intense," he said of the trials. "Two hundred swimmers compete in each event, and only two go to the Olympics. You make third place or less, you're a loser. So I choked like ninety percent of the people there and didn't go to the Olympics. I swam well, though, and I'll be ready for it next time."

Josh came in tenth at the trials. Doug Gjertson and Joe Hudepohl won in his events (100- and 200-

meter freestyle) and went to the Olympics. Though they were both finalists, neither medaled.

Josh's team didn't win the national championship either. Stanford, the school Josh almost went to, began a streak of NCAA championships that would continue through 1994.

Josh calls 1993 his "blessing year." "I was undefeated in the dual-meet season where we race other colleges. I won in the 200 free (1:34.2), 200 individual medley (1:45.5), 200 butterfly (1:45.6), 200 backstroke (1:46.0). I lost the 200 back one time."

That year culminated in another conference championship and Josh's first title in individual events in the NCAA.

Of that title Josh says, "In the NCAAs, I won the 200 free, and was a finalist in the IM (individual medley) and 200 fly."

It was an amazing year for Josh, and he hopes to repeat it as he faces the Olympic Trials this coming year.

In 1994, Josh was a member of the winning and record-breaking (American and NCAA) 400-yard relay team. The finals was quite a race. Stanford was ahead the whole way, but in the last twenty-five yards Josh's team caught up and touched them out. The time was 2:51.0.

All looked well until Josh suffered a big upset in the 200-yard free. He didn't even place in the top three.

"It was one of those teachable moments," Josh says. "God was able to teach me some things. He's not so much concerned with my success as my character. I had a fifth-place finish even though I was ranked number one in the nation. It would have been easy to sulk. In the same meet, I was able to come back and do a lifetime best on the relay (42.1) by almost a second. I call it the Holy Spirit swim."

This past year Josh represented the United States at the Pan American Games. He also turned professional. He still trains with the UT team, but represents the national team at swim meets. During the school year, the national team races other colleges; in the summer, they travel twice to other countries.

In the fall of 1994 Josh traveled to Rome with the national team and swam on a 400 freestyle relay team that missed the world record of 3:16.5 by four-tenths of a second. Their 3:16.9 did set a new meet record, though. And in the spring of 1995, in Buenos Aires, Argentina, Josh was a three-time gold medalist, capturing the 400 freestyle (3:55) and both freestyle relays, the 400 and the 800.

Then came August 1995 and one of the most exciting times of his life. In a meet in Fukuoka, Japan, Josh gold-medaled in the 400 free, the 4 X 100 free, the 4 X 100 medley, and the 4 X 200 free relays.

That 4 X 200 was a real corker. Josh set a lifetime best time in it because he was the lead-off swimmer. (The lead-off swimmer is the only one who actually sets an individual time.) In fact, he had the best time in the world for 1995: 1:48.4.

This past year, he started to build relationships with his teammates to begin sharing Christ with them. Josh comments on the period following the Fukuoka meet: "The first several weeks it was my focus to build relationships. And God really added credibility to my Christian testimony at the end of the trip when He allowed me to swim those spectacular swims. I got to be flag bearer for the U.S. delegation at the games. It was very exciting and humbling. I felt during that time how fortunate we are to live in a great country like the USA, and how much God has blessed us. We're living off the blessings that have been passed on down."

What are Josh's chances of making the 1996 Summer Olympics? He is ranked first in the world in the 200-meter free. That means in the Olympics he could swim in the 200-meter free, 4 X 200 free relay, and 4 X 100 free relay.

"Last year I was fifth in the country in the 200. They take four for the relays and two alternates. My coach's philosophy is that each year you have to do something harder to get faster. This year I'm doing more yardage and with greater intensity. I'm swimming some of the fastest times I ever have. So I think my chances are good."

How does Josh's faith work next to his sport?

"I have to remind myself that God isn't as concerned about my success as my character. Now that I am His son, He won't give me a platform that my character can't handle. It's been my prayer for a couple of years now that God would continue to mold me and make me the man of God He wants me to be, and whatever platform He gives me, I'll use it for His glory. Because I know it can all be taken away in the blink of an eye."

That attitude goes far in life as well as sports. So more power to you, Josh Davis, and hope you make it to Atlanta in 1996.

Don't miss out
on the other books
in the Sports Heroes series!

Sports Heroes: Baseball
0-310-49551-2
$4.99

Smashing a winning home run in the ninth inning of a World Series game. Baseball fans dream of it. Joe Carter has done it. Find out what it's like in *Sports Heroes: Baseball*. Plus, meet Orel Hershiser, who pitched 59 consecutive no-run innings—and other great players who share with you the excitement, challenges, and secrets of becoming a major-league star.

Sports Heroes: Basketball
0-310-49561-X
$4.99

Take to the court with some of the NBA's best players. This action-packed book puts you right in the game! Score almost at will with Mark Price's offensive power. Bury opponents with the deadly three-point accuracy of Hersey Hawkins. And find out what some of the greatest stars do *off* the court as well as on it. Here's a thorough look at what it takes to make it in basketball today.

Sports Heroes: Football
0-310-49571-7
$4.99

Go head-to-head with some of the greatest players and coaches in the NFL. *Sports Heroes: Football* will let you taste last-minute victory through Roger Staubach's famous two-minute offense, take you on-field with defensive giant Reggie White, and show you the ins and outs of NFL stardom through the eyes of some of football's biggest stars.

Sports Heroes: Track and Field
0-310-49581-4
$4.99

What would it be like to race world-record-setter Carl Lewis—and win? Leroy Burrell, the runner who beat Lewis to become the fastest man in the world, can tell you. He's just one of the champions you'll meet in *Sports Heroes: Track and Field*—heroes like decathlete Dave Johnson, who won an Olympic medal despite a broken foot. Find out from them what it takes to reach the Olympics in track and field.

Sports Heroes: Soccer
0-310-20264-7
$4.99

Step onto the soccer field with Desmond Armstrong and see what it's like to join the best players on the planet in the World All-Star Game. Meet Brian Davidson, Jon Payne, Scott Cook, and other soccer greats. Discover their best moves . . . and let them show you exactly what it takes to become a professional soccer player today.

Sports Heroes: Summer Olympics
0-310-20266-3
$4.99

Track with Carl Lewis through his stunning career as a four-time Olympian. Find out how Jacqueline Joyner-Kersee overcame a strained tendon to achieve a double-win at the 1988 Olympics. Learn about the victories and setbacks of some of the world's greatest Olympic athletes. They'll inspire you to be the finest athlete you can be!

Sports Heroes: Basketball 2
0-310-20265-5
$4.99

How does David Robinson snuff the hottest shooters in the NBA? Let him tell you himself! Meet Julius Erving and Kevin Johnson. Share with A. C. Green the joy of winning a championship over Larry Bird and the Celtics. All this—and much more—is here in *Sports Heroes: Basketball 2*.

Sports Heroes: Baseball 2
0-310-20263-9
$4.99

Only a few incredible players ever join the ranks of baseball's 30/30 Club. Head for the field with Howard Johnson, who's made the club three times! Plus, meet grand-slam phenom Matt Nokes, 1993 Rookie of the Year Tim Salmon, pitcher Scott Sanderson, and other baseball heroes—up close and in action, in *Sports Heroes: Baseball 2*.

The Sports Heroes Series is available
at fine bookstores everywhere.

ZondervanPublishingHouse
Grand Rapids, Michigan
http://www.zondervan.com

A Division of HarperCollins*Publishers*

America Online
AOL Keyword:zon